★THE★ THREE LITTLE PIGS

These are the three little pigs.

The time has come for them
to set out on their own.

The first little pig
builds her house out of
STRAW.

The second little
pig builds her
house out of
STICKS.

The third little pig wants her house to be STRONG, so she builds hers out of BRICKS.

Suddenly, a big bad wolf appears in search of food. He comes to the door of the first little pig's house.

THEN I'LL HUFF AND I'LL PUFF AND I'LL BLOW YOUR HOUSE IN!

The wolf takes a deep breath . . .

and the straw house

TUMBLES DOWN.

The first little pig scurries to safety in the house of sticks.

LITTLE PIGS,
LITTLE PIGS,
LET ME IN!

NOT BY THE
HAIR OF MY
CHINNY CHIN
CHIN!

THEN I'LL HUFF AND
I'LL PUFF AND I'LL ...

The two little pigs escape to their sister's brick house, but the wolf follows them.

But try as he might . . .

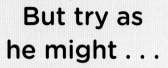

HUFF

PUFF

GRRR!

the wolf could not blow down the house of bricks.

So he climbed on the roof and slid down the chimney instead!

The wolf was NOT expecting the pot of boiling water at the bottom!

The three little pigs
never saw that big
bad wolf again.

PENGUIN BOOKS
An imprint of Penguin Random House LLC, New York

Text © 2020 by Penguin Random House LLC
Illustrations © 2020 by Carly Gledhill

Visit us online at penguinrandomhouse.com
Manufactured in China • 1 2 3 4 5 6 7 8 9 10
Special Markets ISBN 9780593352854 Not for Resale
Cover design by Maggie Edkins

This Imagination Library edition is published by Penguin Young Readers, a division
of Penguin Random House, exclusively for Dolly Parton's Imagination Library,
a not-for-profit program designed to inspire a love of reading and learning, sponsored
in part by The Dollywood Foundation. Penguin's trade editions of this work are
available wherever books are sold.